THE GREAT ENCOUNTER:
A Special Meeting Before Columbus

by

Patricia A. Piercy

SKILL BUILDING SECTION
by
Charlotte J. DeWitty

African American IMAGES

1991
CHICAGO, ILLINOIS

Cover Illustration by Napoleon Wilkerson
Illustrations by Napoleon Wilkerson

First edition, second printing

DEDICATION

THIS BOOK IS DEDICATED
TO MY CHILDREN,
SONASHA CHERICE AND
ASA JABARI
WITH MUCH LOVE

ACKNOWLEDGEMENTS

The Author wishes to thank Dr. Ivan Van Sertima for his scholarly and extensive research regarding the African presence in America published in his book, "They Came Before Columbus" by Random House in 1976. I also wish to express my deep appreciation to my daughter, Sonasha and my nephew Bryson DeWitty for their unending, astute questions about his book which provided the inspiration to write "The Great Encounter." To Temujin, Pittsburgh's own African priest and storyteller, I express my gratitude for the use of his name.

The author extends much appreciation to Charlotte Piercy DeWitty for writing the "Skill Building" section of the book and especially for her encouragement and suggestions throughout the writing of the manuscript. Finally, many thanks to Beverly Braxton for her editing of the manuscript and to Saundra Evans for embellishing the "Skill Building" section. To my husband, Earl Braxton, thank you for your constant support and nudging to express myself in writing.

THE GREAT ENCOUNTER:
A Special Meeting Before Columbus

Patricia A. Piercy

Illustrations by Napoleon Wilkerson

SKILL BUILDING SECTION
by
Charlotte J. DeWitty

"Look out!", shouted Bryson to Sonasha as she swiftly darted around the tree.

"Oh no!", screamed Shaun and Kirsten. Sonasha, Shaun, Bryson and Kirsten were having a delightful time playing some of their favorite games. Now it was Shaun's turn to get in the center of the ring. Who will catch him? Will it be Sonasha, Kirsten or galloping Bryson? No one wanted to be in the center of the ring and caught in the clutches of the Protruding Octopus. Just as Shaun was about to get swept up by the Octopus' arms, the bell rang for school to begin.

The children hurriedly picked up their bookbags, ran to their classrooms, and excitedly waited for the first class to begin. They knew today was a special day because their teacher had invited an African priest and storyteller to the class. Mrs. Johnson, their teacher, had told them that the storyteller Temujin, had a spectacular story for them.

The boys and girls were curious and trying their best to guess what the story was about. Sonasha, who loves to read books about Africa, whispered to Shaun, "I'm sure he'll tell us an African folktale."

Shaun, who loved to play tricks on his classmates, declared, "No, he's going to fool us. He's not going to tell us a story at all, he's going to teach us how to play the Talking Drums."

Bryson, who has always wanted to become an astronaut, stated firmly, "He'll tell us about space travel and establishing cultures on other planets."

Finally, Kirsten, the class critic on every animated cartoon teasingly insisted, "The story is about my favorite cartoon, 'The Little Mermaid'."

The children continued talking back and forth. Then suddenly a hush fell over the room as Mrs. Johnson entered. Next to her was a tall, stately man with a broad smile, erect shoulders, dressed in colorful African garb, carrying a long wood-carved cane. He strode to the center of the classroom. Although he was walking quickly, it seemed like an eternity for the children. They knew this must be Temujin and could not wait for him to begin.

Sonasha's eyes were as huge as saucers. Shaun and Bryson's arms rapidly flung back and forth attempting to get Temujin's attention. Kirsten scooted so close to the edge of her seat to get a better view of Temujin that she toppled onto the floor.

The children, Temujin and Mrs. Johnson laughed so hard that the room seemed to shake. Then Temujin tapped his cane on the floor three times and in a deep voice commanded, "Listen, my children, I always begin my stories with questions, for it is through the questions that the story is told, so listen carefully. The first question is: Have you ever discovered anything?"

Shaun quickly answered, "Yes, I discovered some bugs in my backyard."

"What did you do with them?" asked Temujin.

"I put them in a jar and asked my mom if I could keep them in my room."

"What did your mom say about that?" asked Temujin.

Shaun responded, "Mom yelled and said, 'Get those things out of here right now!' Then she counted to ten. She said that I could look at the bugs for a little while and then let them go. Mom said bugs had as much right as anybody else to live and enjoy the earth. She said that if I kept them in the jar they would certainly die."

"My dear son, your mother is a wise woman," replied Temujin. "Now for my second question. If you were travelling and you came upon an island with people on it who looked and acted different from you what would you want to know about them, and how would you feel?"

"I'd ask them if they had ever seen 'The Little Mermaid'," Kirsten replied immediately.

"I'd feel a little nervous about meeting somebody new, but after I got to know them, I'd ask them to play space travel games with me," Bryson chimed in.

Shaun added, "I'd want to know if the children played tricks on their parents or if their parents made them eat green beans or made them go to bed at ..."

Sonasha interrupted, "I'd wonder about how they live, if they ever had other visitors and if they had books about themselves and about us. I would wonder what they thought about us."

The boys and girls looked puzzled as they tried to think of Temujin's next question. Temujin then said, "Now my children my final question before I begin the story is: Who discovered America?"

"Why everybody knows Columbus discovered America in 1492," responded Bryson immediately.

"No he didn't discover America," interrupted Shaun quickly, "that's what we've always been taught." Well no one could tell if Shaun was serious or playing another one of his tricks!

"If we were taught it in school, it's got to be true," replied Bryson.

Sonasha boasted, "Well I have a book that says ten people discovered America!"

Kirsten waved her hand so that she could get Temujin's attention, "Wait a minute, wait a minute, I just saw a cartoon about Columbus' voyages to the New World and why we celebrate Columbus Day!" she exclaimed.

The children continued the lively discussion until Mrs. Johnson said, "Children, I need your attention. Put on your critical- thinking caps. I think they must have fallen off your heads," she said jokingly.

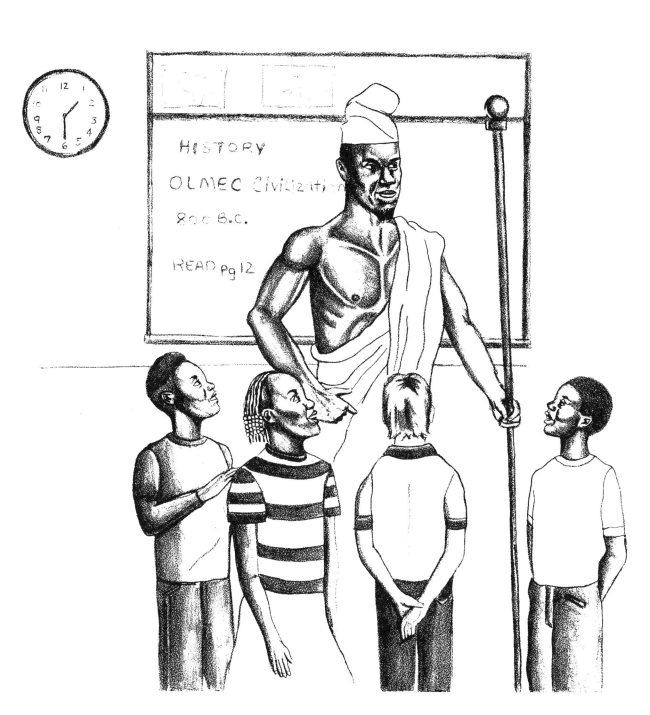

Mrs. Johnson knew that she had a group of very critical thinkers. She knew that if she asked the right questions it would move their thoughts in places and directions that their thinking had not gone before. She then asked, "Was there anyone in America before Columbus came to America and exactly what did Columbus discover?"

The boys and girls thought about this question and suddenly Sonasha exclaimed, "Well wait a minute, how on earth did Columbus or any of those other men discover America if there were already Native Americans living here before Columbus arrived?"

Kirsten thoughtfully responded, "That would be like a Native American, let's call him Chief Clearwater, going to Spain in 1492 and saying he discovered Spain and then every year the Spaniards would celebrate Chief Clearwater Day!" Of course, everyone laughed at Kirsten's comment.

Shaun, considering all that had been said, commented, "You know, you've really got a point there. Anyway, if he discovered America why was it already named America before he came?"

"Anyway, all of the books I've read talk about the highly-developed Native Americans long before Columbus came," Sonasha added.

"You are all so right and this is so puzzling to me. Who then was Columbus, what did he do and why have we been taught that he discovered America?" Bryson asked, looking quite confused. Both Temujin and Mrs. Johnson looked at each other, thankful for the children's curiosity. Temujin nodded to Mrs. Johnson, signaling her to answer the question.

"Columbus came to America and discovered what Europeans did not already know. They were not certain that the Americas existed. Columbus was a very determined, tireless man. He was also very selfish and greedy. In my opinion, his greediness led him not to tell about various African artifacts he found and Africans whom he saw when he did come to the Americas. What really matters here today children, is that long before Columbus set sail for America, Africans had first come to America not as slaves but as traders, explorers, and visitors and with the Native Americans built a great civilization. That is the message I'd like to leave you with today. Now Temujin has that spectacular story for you," ended Mrs. Johnson.

The children were amazed by Mrs. Johnson's answer. They knew Native Americans were here before Columbus but they didn't know about Africans. They wanted to hear more from Temujin.

Temujin was deep in thought. He wanted the children to know that Africans made significant contributions to the development of America. He also wanted them to know that any person or nation discovering a civilization is as foolish as Kirsten had so well pointed out.

The children, in their eagerness to hear more from Temujin, began to chant, "Temujin, Temujin, we want Temujin, tell us a story."

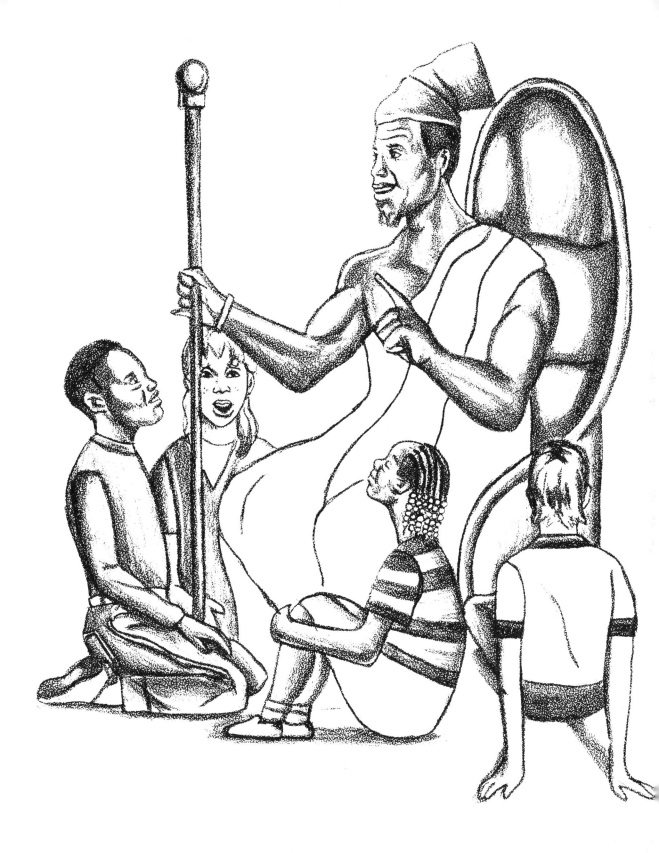

PART II

The children's chanting jolted Temujin from his thoughts as he heard them begging him to tell them about one of the journeys Africans made to the Americas. He decided to tell the story of the "Great Encounter." He tapped his cane on the floor three times to command the children's attention and said, "Listen my children, I will tell a story of long ago, a story which my great-great-grandfather told to me which was told to him by his great-great-grandfather, who was the keeper of history for his African clan." The children excitedly gathered around Temujin and he began to tell a most glorious tale.

"It was just before dawn. The sun's rays slowly began to peek over the hillside showing the brilliant colors of the hilly countryside. Everything was so peaceful and calm, so quiet that you could hear the gentle winds from the Priest's chambers."

"Everyone in the chambers seemed to be sleeping peacefully except for Ade', Priest Jabari's son. Ade' was gazing out the window. He knew today was the day of departure for the other world far, far away. He remembered the conversation several months ago between his father, Priest Jabari and his father's advisor, Mwanza. Mwanza told him that the huge sea was at times so dangerous that no ships could escape the huge waves or it could be so calm that ships could stand still forever — either way no one would survive."

"Ade' turned from the window and looked at his father, who seemed to be restless. He could tell that his father was worried even as he slept. He could tell by the funny way his muscle jumped out of his arm and the way one eyebrow kept moving up and down. Ade' had a lot of faith in his father. Priest Jabari was known throughout the kingdom to be a courageous, wise man who loved to explore and find ways to meet the challenges of any situation. Ade' was thrilled and proud to be going with his father on this journey. Ade's job would be to alert his father's crew when the first sign of land was in sight."

"Ade' was the only boy permitted to go on the journey. He was known throughout the kingdom to be brave like his father, but Ade' did not believe he was brave. Often he felt scared and afraid inside, but was too embarrassed to tell anyone. Today, he felt particularly afraid. He was not worried about the voyage. Something else worried him. He wondered if the faraway land had children and what they were like. Would he be able to talk with them, play games and sing songs with them? Would he understand them and would they understand him? Would they become friends?"

"Ade's thoughts were interrupted as he heard the drums roll announcing that it was time to rise and prepare to set sail on the long journey. Ade' and Priest Jabari along with several other men and women walked aboard the ships. Families said goodbye, prayers were completed and the fleet slowly departed, leaving behind the beautiful countryside. Ade' was sad and excited. He was sad about leaving his mother and friends behind, but excited about going on the voyage."

"Throughout the entire voyage, Ade' had a deep abiding faith that his father's fleet would arrive safely in the New World. Even when the rains poured heavily and winds were spinning the ships round and round, he knew his father would bravely direct the crew and they would arrive safely. He continued to worry about meeting new children in the faraway land."

"One day while eating with his father, Ade' nervously said, 'Father, I am afraid. I am worried about meeting the other children from this faraway land. What if they don't like me? What if I don't understand them and they don't understand me?'

"Ade's father walked over to him, placed his hands on his shoulders and said, 'my son it takes courage to admit when one is afraid, that makes you courageous and wise because you know when you are afraid. I too have felt afraid about this journey and meeting new people. When I feel that way, I remember the advice your grandfather gave to me which I shall now pass on to you. He said: my son when you meet another, meet face to face, look eye to eye, greet with respect and honor in your heart, let no harm come to you or the other and share the love in your heart.'

"Ade' and his father hugged. Ade' clung to his father's waist for several minutes. He felt his father's warm tears slowly dripping onto the top of his head. Ade' was quite moved. He never knew that his father was also afraid."

"For several months, his father's words kept spinning in his head. He began to feel them in his heart and that worried, scared feeling began to slowly fade away."

"Early one morning many months after the fleet left from the Western coast of Africa, Ade' was staring across the sea,day-dreaming about his new friends. Gradually, he began to see trees and a hillside. He leaped from the bench on deck and shouted, 'We've arrived, We've arrived!' As the fleet slowly began to approach the harbor, Ade' could feel his heart beating faster and faster. He felt a mixture of excitement, fear and courage. He looked toward his father and remembered his advice and took a deep breath of the morning air almost as if he were breathing in the words of advice from his father."

"Meanwhile, on the harbor stood Chief Ottawa and his son, Coyote. They were both slowly walking toward the edge of the land. It seemed almost as if they were expecting the fleet. Ade' noticed Coyote immediately. He noticed his long, straight, black hair and the beautiful band of cloth and feathers around his head. He also was entranced by his deep, large, dark eyes. Coyote noticed Ade's silky, black skin, and kinky, black hair and the beautiful white cloth that covered his entire body. Ade' recognized that Coyote spoke a different language as he heard him say something to the Chief.

Yet both felt a deep and strong sense of connection, a kindred spirit, a oneness between them. Chief Ottawa and Priest Jabari's eyes met as they stood directly facing each other. Coyote and Ade' stood before each other, their eyes locked, they felt tremendous respect and love. From their eyes poured tears of joy for each boy knew they had found a friend forever and with this thought, the boys hugged. Chief Ottawa and Priest Jabari bowed to each other. The men and women on the ships exited and began a life in the New World.''

"This Great Encounter and many others like it brought together two different peoples, African and Native American, who had respect for each other, respect for the elders and ancestors, respect for the land and sea and for all of nature."

The children were so fascinated by the story that they did not hear the announcement that it was time for recess. Mrs. Johnson came to the front of the classroom and said, "Children, Temujin must go now and visit other classrooms."

The boys and girls asked Temujin to stay longer and to tell more stories. They even invited him to play with them at recess.

"I would be most happy to return," replied Temujin, "but before I go, I have some homework for you. You are to write the lessons you have learned today. You are also to tell this story to your family and friends. Then you will be on your way to becoming great storytellers."

The children excitedly accepted the offer and ran out to the playground with Temujin behind them. Temujin left the classroom, so very thankful to be a part of such a wonderful group of children. He knew he would return to tell many more stories. During recess, he was caught in the Octopus' arms and the children felt they had met a grand African priest and storyteller and had also made a wonderful friend.

THE END

NOTES TO PARENTS AND TEACHERS

1. The story told by Temujin, *The Great Encounter,* is based on a voyage reportedly made by Abubakari II, a Malian Emperor who led a fleet of 2,000 ships to America in 1311. (Van Sertima, 1976).

2. For the most part, it has been assumed that America lived isolated from the rest of the world and developed all of its cultures independently until Columbus came. Recently this myth has been seriously questioned. (Van Sertima, 1976, pg. 54).

3. "... the whole notion of any race (European, African or American) discovering a full-blown civilization is absurd .... They presume some innate superiority in the 'discoverer' and something inferior and barbaric in the people 'discovered' ..." (Van Sertima, 1976, pg. 255).

4. The most definitive compelling work on African presence in America is Ivan Van Sertima's book, *They Came Before Columbus* (1976). In this work, Van Sertima researches numerous disciplines and applies a critical and stringent test to his findings. He clearly shows the African presence and legacy in ancient America. The African presence in America is evidenced through artistic and cultural influences, similarities in socio-religious beliefs and practices, botanical and linguistic data, and through reports and observations by European travellers and documents of East and West Africa. Van Sertima has demonstrated that long before Columbus' voyages, Africans came first to America as explorers, traders and visitors and with the Native Americans built a great civilization that could not be erased. He has made a significant contribution to the rescue and reconstruction of Black history and humanity.

5. In Maulana Karenga's book, *Introduction to Black Studies*, (1989, pgs. 74-77), he summarizes Van Sertima's findings regarding the major evidence supporting African presence, influence and achievement before the coming of Columbus.

REFERENCES

1. Karenga, Maulana, (1982) *Introduction to Black Studies*, University of Sankore Press, Los Angeles, California.

2. Van Sertima, Ivan, (1976) *They Came Before Columbus*, Random House, Inc., New York, New York.

SKILL BUILDING
ACTIVITIES

SKILL BUILDING ACTIVITIES

How To Best Utilize The Skill Building Activities

The skill building section of this book is designed to emphasize writing, critical reading and thinking skills, vocabulary skills, problem solving and predicting skills through a series of activities. These activities may be done alone by your child or with you. We do encourage parent/ family participation and that it is kept interesting and fun. Your child may choose to do some of the activities or all of them. Below are some helpful hints to assist your child.

1. After reading the story, have your child retell the story.

2. Before working on the "Critical Thinking Cap Game" discuss the questions orally with your child. You may want to provide a spiral notebook or paper so that writing and drawing is not restricted.

3. With the "Vocabulary" activity, divide the words into three groups. Have your child study and learn the meanings of one group at a time. Another game to play is having your child act out some of the words.

4. There are several fun approaches to doing the "So Many Words" game. Here are just a few.

    (1) You and your child take turns naming words.
    (2) See how many words your child can write in a limited period of time.
    (3) Have a contest between you and your child to see how many words you can write.
    (4) Invite other family members to participate.

5. Pretend you are Ade' about to make a trip to a new land. Make a list of three feelings you would have about leaving most of your family and going on a long voyage.

(1) _____(2) _____(3) _____

On a separate sheet of paper draw three different pictures of you describing the feelings you listed.

6. What was Mrs. Johnson's message to the children about Columbus? Give details from the story to support your answer.

_____

_____

_____

7. Let's suppose Priest Jabari and Ade' were selfish, mean, and disrespectful. Write a paragraph predicting what happened after they got off the ship.

_____

_____

_____

8. On a separate sheet of paper draw your favorite scene from the story.

9. Why was Ade' so worried about meeting new children?

_____

_____

What are some of the feelings you've had about meeting new children?

_____

10. What would you do if you were worried about meeting new children?

_____

_____

_____

11. On a separate sheet of paper, draw a picture about what happened after Coyote and Ade' began living together in America. Write a paragraph about your picture.

_____

_____

_____

12. Choose one of the characters, Sonasha, Bryson, Shaun or Kirsten. Write a story about what that person told their family about Temujin's story.

_____

_____

_____

_____

_____

_____

_____

_____

_____

_____

_____

THE "CRITICAL THINKING CAP" GAME

1. What is the main idea of "The Great Encounter?"

_____

_____

_____

2. Who was your favorite character in the story? Tell why that character was your favorite.

_____

_____

3. On a separate sheet of paper, draw a picture of what Ade' saw as their ship came close to America.

_____

_____

4. Pretend you are Coyote. Write a paragraph telling what Coyote and his father, Chief Ottawa were talking about as they saw the ship coming to the land.

_____

_____

_____

SEQUENCING
"THE GREAT ENCOUNTER"

Number the sentences in the order that they happened in the story.

_____   Temujin asked the children lots of questions.

_____   The children were outside playing a game.

_____   Ade' told his father how worried he was.

_____   Chief Ottawa and his son, Coyote, greeted Priest Jabari and his son, Ade'.

_____   Temujin and the children played a game.

_____   Priest Jabari's ship left for America.

_____   Temujin and Mrs. Johnson walked into the classroom.

WRITING SKILLS

Use the following key words to tell the order of Part I of the story.

1. First, _____

_____

2. Next, _____

_____

3. Then, _____

_____

4. After that, _____

_____

5. Finally, _____

_____

Use the following key words to tell the order of Part II of the story.

1. First, _____

_____

2. Next, _____

_____

3. Then, _____

_____

4. After that, _____

_____

5. Finally, _____

_____

VOCABULARY

Below are some words that were used in the story "The Great Encounter."
Learn the meaning of each word and be able to use each in a sentence.

1. greedy	7. survive	13. arrived
2. stately	8. swiftly	14. respect
3. garb	9. delightful	15. selfish
4. chant	10. discovered	16. kingdom
5. voyage	11. clan	17. ancestors
6. curiosity	12. entranced	18. determined

"THE GREAT ENCOUNTER"

CROSSWORD PUZZLE

ACROSS

2. talk softly
6. have a high regard for
8. be the first to find
9. lovely, pretty

DOWN

1. asking why
3. having great meaning, influence or value
4. calm and quite
5. quickly
7. to fall forward
10. relatives who lived a long time ago.

ancestor   beautiful   discover   important   peaceful
question   rapidly   respect   topple   whisper

8

SO MANY WORDS

Using two letters or more, how many words can you make using the letters in the word

TEMUJIN

_____

_____

_____

_____

_____

_____

_____

_____

_____

_____

_____

_____

HIDDEN WORDS FROM

"THE GREAT ENCOUNTER"

```
C O L O O H C S S E L F I S H Y X F
I O A E M Q U L H F M E S S A G E M
V G N A A E L Q O S T V C D W E X L
I R G V B R G I B M A F O I L N C C
L E U E E H N L I S T E N S U C I H
I E A M R R D J Y K T E N C F O T I
Z D G B E E S M R U E L E O K U E L
A Y E R S U H A O L N I C V N U M D
T C M A P W I P T S T N T E A T E R
I N H C E F P S S I I G I R H E N E
O S G E C A S T T Y O Z O E T R T N
N T F D T F C V X A N N N D B A L D
```

Can you find the words below hidden in the above word game?
Words may be horizontal, vertical or diagonal.

ATTENTION	ENCOUNTER	MESSAGE
CHILDREN	EXCITEMENT	RESPECT
CIVILIZATION	FEELING	SCHOOL
CONNECTION	GREEDY	SELFISH
CONVERSATION	LANGUAGE	SHIPS
DISCOVERED	LEARN	STORY
EMBRACED	LISTEN	THANKFUL

"THE GREAT ENCOUNTER"
ANSWERS

CROSSWORD PUZZLE

SEQUENCING ANSWERS

3, 1, 5, 6, 7, 4, 2

HIDDEN WORDS ANSWERS

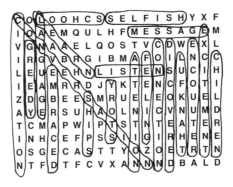